Katharina Grossmann-Hensel

# Papa is a Pirate

the biggest,

the strongest,

and the bravest

**NorthSouth**
New York / London

"**R**ough seas today!" says Papa when he gets home from work. "Waves like monsters."

"Rough seas?" I ask. "At your office?"

"What a storm!" says Papa. "If you only knew . . ."

"Knew what?" I ask him.

Papa leans in close to my ear and whispers so it tickles, "Shhhh. Your papa is a *pirate*!"

"How can you be a pirate?" I ask. "You have a bicycle, not a boat!"

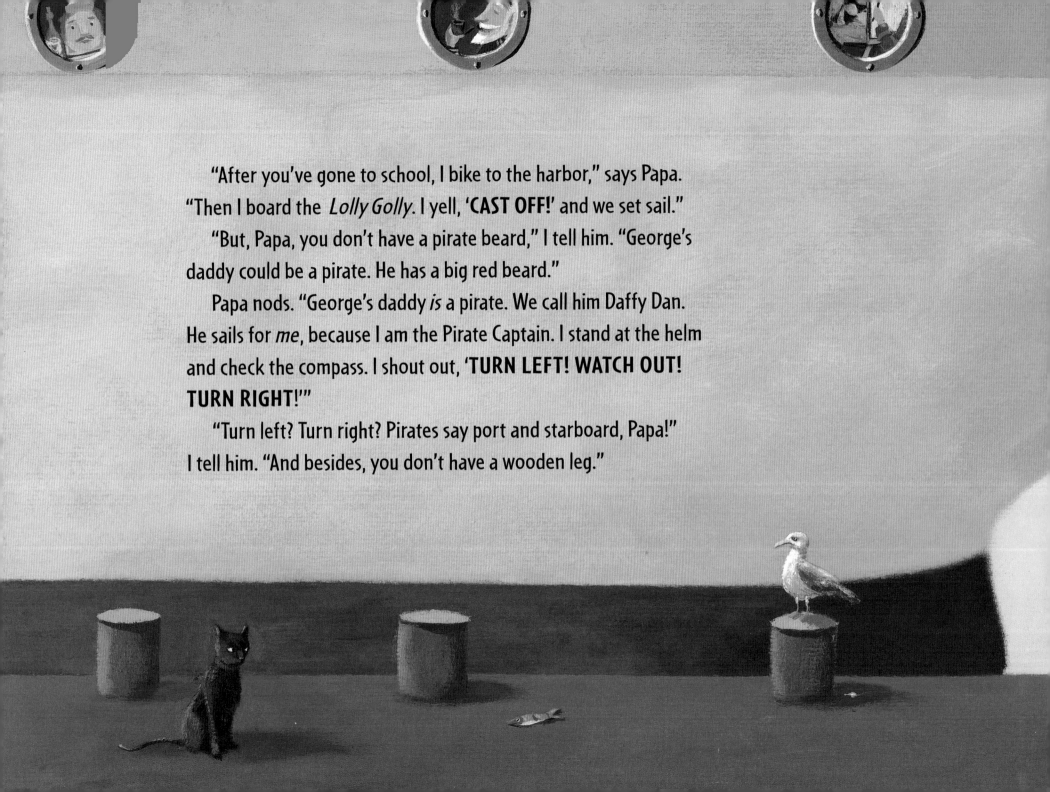

"After you've gone to school, I bike to the harbor," says Papa. "Then I board the *Lolly Golly*. I yell, **'CAST OFF!'** and we set sail."

"But, Papa, you don't have a pirate beard," I tell him. "George's daddy could be a pirate. He has a big red beard."

Papa nods. "George's daddy *is* a pirate. We call him Daffy Dan. He sails for *me*, because I am the Pirate Captain. I stand at the helm and check the compass. I shout out, **'TURN LEFT! WATCH OUT! TURN RIGHT!'**"

"Turn left? Turn right? Pirates say port and starboard, Papa!" I tell him. "And besides, you don't have a wooden leg."

"A wooden leg is a nuisance," says Papa. "Only pirates on TV have wooden legs. A *real* pirate has a stubbly chin like mine and a bird like our Petey."

"A parakeet?" I say. "Pirates have **PARROTS**, not parakeets."

"Ah, yes," says Papa. "But in his heart, Petey *is* a parrot."

"All he ever says is, 'Thank you,'" I tell Papa.

"Not on board," says Papa. "Why, just yesterday, while Daffy Dan was scrubbing the deck, Petey squawked, 'Avast there, ye landlubber! Yo ho ho!'"

"Oh, Papa, I don't believe it," I say.

"It's all true," says Papa.

"Then what do you do all day long?" I ask.

"When I'm not keeping watch through my telescope, I write messages and float them off to you in bottles. I've sent you hundreds. Haven't you gotten them?"

"No," I say. "Just some postcards sometimes."

"That's the trouble with messages in bottles," says Papa. "You never know just where they'll land. That's why I write you postcards too."

"What's there to eat on board your ship?" I ask.

"Well, Daffy Dan sits on the bow and fishes,"
says Papa.

"You don't *like* fish!" I remind him.

"Not a problem," says Papa. "He never catches any.
We have instant soup with salty seawater instead.
And we keep a cow on board for milk. We have two
camels too."

"Camels? On a pirate ship?"

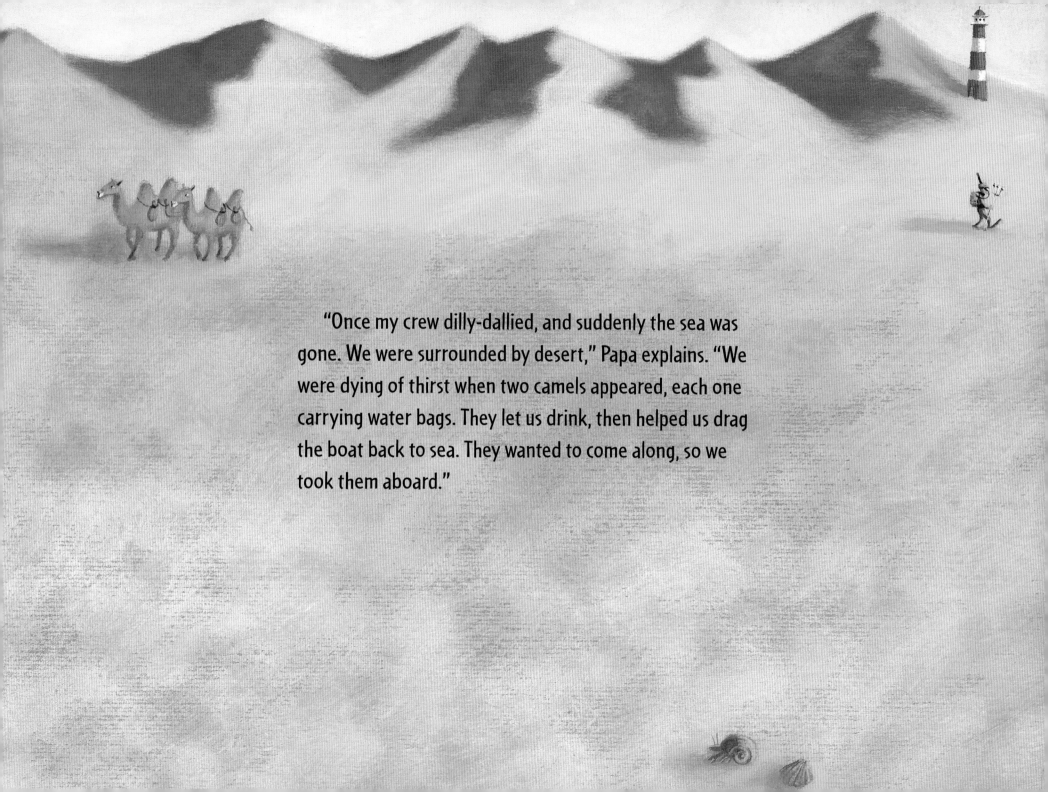

"Once my crew dilly-dallied, and suddenly the sea was gone. We were surrounded by desert," Papa explains. "We were dying of thirst when two camels appeared, each one carrying water bags. They let us drink, then helped us drag the boat back to sea. They wanted to come along, so we took them aboard."

"How do you make money if you don't go to the office?" I ask.

"We put on pirate shows for cruise ships," says Papa. "We walk the plank and I yell, 'All men over the board!'"

"Men *overboard*," I correct him.

"Ah, yes. Well, we splash around, and sometimes I even dare to walk the anchor line! Tourists pay a lot for a good pirate show."

"Do you ever sleep on the *Lolly Golly*?" I ask.

"Certainly," says Papa. "A pirate must be prepared to sleep anywhere."

"Do you sleep in your cabin, then?" I ask.

"No way!" says Papa. "I sleep out under the stars. They are the best compass and guide my way."

"One night, after steering by the stars, I discovered an island,"
Papa goes on. "It was so tiny, it had only one birch tree on it. And
can you guess who was sitting under that birch tree? Your mother,
that's who! Mom is a pirate too. Her ship had sunk, and she'd swum
all by herself across half an ocean, surrounded by sharks. She was
in a mighty bad mood when I found her."

"You told me before that Mom was a princess," I remind him.
"Oh, she's that too," says Papa. "She became a pirate after
she'd conquered all her kingdom's dragons."

"Do you ever have to fight other pirates?"
I ask Papa.

"Of course!" Papa tells me. "Every third
Thursday at six o'clock there is a Big Pirate
Battle. Cannons boom, water splashes, boats
rock. Everyone yells. The winner gets a gold
trophy cup."

"Is there sword fighting too?" I ask.

"I try to avoid any swordplay," says Papa.
"Too dangerous. I prefer hunting for treasure.
Much safer—though beginners need to watch
out for sea monsters."

"Sea monsters? You've seen a sea monster?"
I ask.

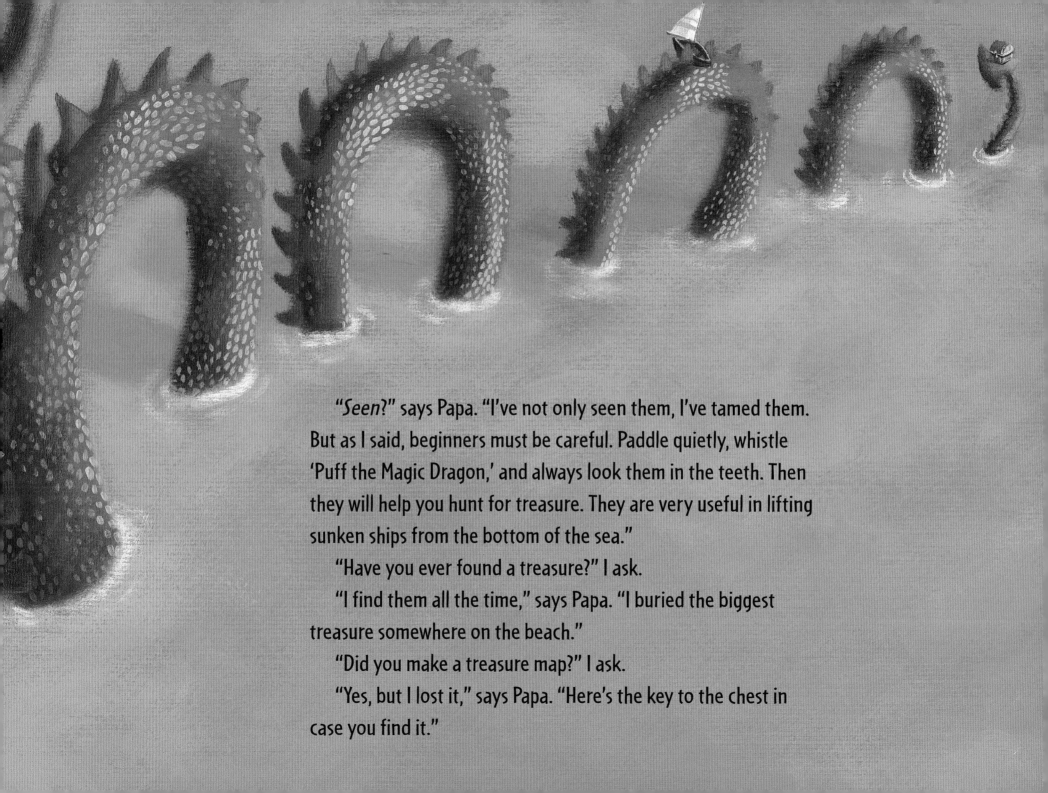

"*Seen*?" says Papa. "I've not only seen them, I've tamed them. But as I said, beginners must be careful. Paddle quietly, whistle 'Puff the Magic Dragon,' and always look them in the teeth. Then they will help you hunt for treasure. They are very useful in lifting sunken ships from the bottom of the sea."

"Have you ever found a treasure?" I ask.

"I find them all the time," says Papa. "I buried the biggest treasure somewhere on the beach."

"Did you make a treasure map?" I ask.

"Yes, but I lost it," says Papa. "Here's the key to the chest in case you find it."

The key is old and rusty and has a pirate's head for a tag. A real treasure chest key. My papa really *is* a pirate! What about yours?

Does your papa *really* spend all day at the office? Is his chin sometimes prickly? Does he sometimes smell like the sea? Why don't you ask him if he has had a stormy day. Then look at him closely. Maybe the ocean waves will still be reflected in his eyes!